THE
FAR
PAVILIONS
PICTURE
BOOK

The Statesman

JANUARY 3, 1879
(Editorial)

Those of our readers who see the *Englishman* as well as the *Statesman,* saw yesterday morning how exactly we had anticipated what the military theorist of the Viceroy's Councils, was about to propound as the real object of this war. The scientific rectification of the frontier, now at last disclosed to us, is the annexation of Affghanistan pure and simple. We are to take possession of all the Affghan strongholds, upon the pretext that Shere Ali "grossly insulted" us at Ali Musjid:

The positions of Cabul and Candahar, linked by the intermediate positions of Gauzni and Khelat-i-Ghilzi, are mutually supporting. They are the only positions in this part of Asia that are so. They form the true strategical frontier of India and, therefore, the only frontier that can be called strictly scientific

The Amir is in a bad way, if these gentlemen remain in power. It is perfectly clear from whose pen these articles come, and a more cynical outrage upon international good faith and morality, than our imperial course has been is not to be found in history. We deliberately force a quarrel upon the Amir, that we may find a pretext for annexing his country and pushing our frontier to the Oxus. It is now openly avowed by the men at the Viceroy's right hand, that the only scientific rectification of which the frontier admits is the occupation of the Affghan fortresses of Cabul, Gauzni Khelat-i-Ghilzi and Candahar. And so they are at once to be occupied. The passes of the Hindu Khoosh are to be closed, by the strong British forts under smart British officers:

From Cabul a comparatively small force might close the passes at Bamian and Khinjan, where strong forts would be as valuable under smart officers as that of Bard. With Cabul and Candahar both held by the English, we should have no question arising as to the good-will of any one. We should have to depend solely and confessedly on ourselves, and should have, too, the advantage of position and consequently the power of reinforcing Candahar by way of Kurum and Cabul from the army of the Northern Punjab.

THE FAR PAVILIONS PICTURE BOOK

DESIGNED BY DAVID LARKIN
WITH
M. M. KAYE

PENGUIN BOOKS

Penguin Books Ltd, Harmondsworth,
Middlesex, England
Penguin Books, 625 Madison Avenue,
New York, New York 10022, U.S.A.
Penguin Books Australia Ltd, Ringwood,
Victoria, Australia
Penguin Books Canada Ltd, 2801 John Street,
Markham, Ontario, Canada L3R 1B4
Penguin Books (N.Z.) Ltd, 182-190 Wairau Road,
Auckland 10, New Zealand

First published in the U.S.A. by Bantam Books, Inc., and
simultaneously in Great Britain by Penguin
Books, 1979

PRINTED IN THE UNITED STATES OF AMERICA
BY REGENSTEINER PRESS

We are most grateful to the museums, photographic libraries, photographers,
artists and publishers whose work we reproduce in this volume.

THE MANSELL COLLECTION

THE ILLUSTRATED LONDON NEWS

AVINASH PASRICHA

NATIONAL ARMY MUSEUM

MADAN MAHATTA

JOHN RICKETSON-HATT

GOVERNMENT OF INDIA

ART DIRECTORS PHOTO LIBRARY

B. KAYE

D. KAYE

M. M. KAYE

INTRODUCTION

The Far Pavilions struck me immediately as an intensely visual novel. After reading it, one can so easily close one's eyes and allow the imagination to conjure up a wealth of landscapes and scenes, people and places. It suggested to me a path of research through old glass negatives and dusty illustrated books that would culminate in a book of pictures to stand as a companion to the novel.

Thus began *The Far Pavilions Picture Book*. The early plans did not count on the energetic and enthusiastic contribution that was to come from M. M. Kaye and her family. Their archives provided the foundation of the *Picture Book*. Her own talent as an illustrator endowed with a professional eye and as a photographer who recorded 'scenes' for her novel many years before it came to be written, in addition to the pictorial work of her mother and sister, has made this book into a fascinating project for me.

We have set out to produce an evocation of the visual aspects of *The Far Pavilions* that will enhance the reader's enjoyment of the novel, that will stimulate the visual imagination yet never for a moment impede or spoil the imaginative workings of the 'inner eye'.

I hope that we have succeeded.

DAVID LARKIN

FOREWORD

When I was first told that there was a scheme afoot to do a *"Far Pavilions Picture Book"* that would be edited and designed by David Larkin, who gave the enchanting book "Faeries" to a grateful and appreciative public, I was more than excited. The prospect of hunting up old prints, line-engravings, photographs, sketches and drawings of the "Raj", and reliving those days as I did so, was enthralling and I cannot tell you what fun it has been, even though it has involved me in far more hard work than I had imagined when I so merrily accepted. I had not realised then that I would be simultaneously struggling with correcting page-proofs for another novel in addition to coping with the normal this and that of family life – which nowadays includes keeping an eye on grandchildren when no other baby-sitter can be found!

I should like to add my thanks to all those who have lent me photographs or other material for this book. Among them the National Army Museum, the Illustrated London News, Gita Mehta, Brigadier Bill Magan of Sam Browne's Cavalry, Indu and Ashok Dayal, Brigadier Pat Macnamara of the Guides and, of course, my mother and my sister Bets. My thanks too to David, and also to Sarah Teale who managed to organise the typescript, and to my husband, Goff, who had to cope with the mess and muddle that I made in the house while working on the picture book – every room awash with scribbled notes, photographs, sketches, drawings and foolscap, and no place to sit down in comfort or put your feet without treading on some valuable bit of paper. Thank you all! It's been a lot of fun and I hope people who buy the book will get even a quarter as much pleasure out of looking at it as I have had from making of it.

M. M. KAYE

CAMP IN THE HIMALAYAS 1852

"*Ashton Hilary Akbar Pelham-Martyn was born in a camp near the crest of a pass in the Himalayas,
and subsequently christened in a patent canvas bucket.*

*His first cry competed manfully with the snarling call of a leopard on the hillside below, and his first
breath had been a lungful of the cold air that blew down from the far rampart of the mountains,
bringing with it a clean scent of snow and pine-needles to thin the reek of hot lamp-oil, the smell of
blood and sweat, and the pungent odour of pack-ponies.*"

Almost any camp in the mountains would have looked like this one over a century ago.
The Pelham-Martyn's camp would probably have been larger than the one I have drawn
here but their tents would have been of this pattern; exactly like the ones I and my
husband, Goff Hamilton, used when we went camping in the valleys of Kashmir – he to
fish for trout in the rivers while I painted. This picture is, in fact, based on sketches by my
mother of the "Valley of the Glaciers" from a camp site at Sonnamarg in Kashmir, to
which I added the near pine trees in order to make it more like the setting I had in mind
for Ash's birthplace, which in the novel would have been much further south.

from CHAPTER I

LOOKING OUT AT THE SNOWS

"Isobel died twenty-four hours after her son's christening, and was buried by her husband and her husband's friend on the summit of the pass overlooking their tents, the entire camp attending the ceremony with every evidence of grief.
'Ash-Baba', as the baby was known to his foster-mother Sita, and to the entire camp, spent the first eighteen months of his life among the high mountains, and took his first steps on a slippery grass hillside within sight of the towering peak of Nanda Devi and the long range of her attendant snows."

The mountains pictured here lie south of the Sutlej Valley beyond CHINI, and this lovely photograph was taken, while on trek in the 30's by Bill Magan, who was at that time serving in Sam Browne's Cavalry, a famous Indian Army Regiment that was raised by that same Sam Browne who was Commandant of the Corps of Guides from 1863 to 1869, and appears several times in "The Far Pavilions."

from CHAPTER I

". . . leaving the hills behind them the camp turned southward."

In this panoramic view you can see the snow peaks, the foothills and the plains of India, with one of the great rivers whose source lies behind the farthest ranges, winding across the flat-lands towards the sea, and irrigating millions of acres of crop-land on its way. Seen from the air, the distances may seem small, but they are not so from the ground, and in the days before railways and metalled roads, travel was slow, and rivers had to be crossed by ferry or where there were fords, since bridges were few and far between.

from CHAPTER I

COCONUT PALMS AND CANAL SOUTH INDIA

". . . and came at last, by way of Jhansi and Sattara, to the lush greenery and long white beaches
of the Coromandal Coast."

I wish there was enough space in this book to show you more of what the camp would
have seen on their wanderings through India, but since there is not I hope that readers
will one day be able to see these things for themselves. A great deal of it will have
changed since Ash's day, but the coast of Coromandal is still green with forests of
coconut-palms that reflect themselves in lakes and canals and village ponds, and throw
long shadows across the white beaches on which the surf breaks all day.

RANI OF JHANSI

Modern Jhansi is a great railway centre, and its glory has departed. But India will never
forget the beautiful, vengeful Rani of Jhansi, for she has become one of the folk-heroines
of the land. Left widowed and childless by the death of her young husband, she was
deprived of his State and its revenues, and much of her personal possessions, by the
Government of the East India Company, who used as their excuse the iniquitous policy
of Annexation by Lapse. But when the Mutiny broke out in 1857, she took her revenge
by slaughtering the entire British garrison in Jhansi, the women and children as well as
the men, having first induced them to surrender the fort to her on a promise of safe
conduct. Dressed in men's clothes and carrying arms, she led her army against the British,
and was eventually killed in battle. I have based this little picture on the only known
portrait of her – and even that was a posthumous one – and I have given her a helmet
and a chainmail scarf to wear, since she was a fighter to the last. I don't know what that
thing is in her hand, presumably a cup. She carries it in the original picture.

OLD PRINT OF DELHI

"Ashton Hilary Akbar celebrated his fourth birthday in the capital of the Moguls, the walled city of Delhi . . . Uncle Akbar marked the occasion by taking him to pray at the Juma Masjid, the magnificent mosque that the Emperor Shah Jehan had built facing the walls of the Lal Kila, the great 'Red Fort' on the banks of the Jumna River."

This old print of Delhi shows the city as it must have looked at that time, and the artist obviously drew it from somewhere on the walls of the Red Fort. The large building in the distance is the Juma Masjid, and studying this print I realise that the Delhi it portrays is not so very different to the one that I myself knew as a child. The great Mosque has not altered and the flat-roofed, close-packed houses are familiar, as is the Chandni Chowk – Delhi's famous 'Silver Street'. There have been many changes since then but I think Shah Jehan would still recognise his city.

from CHAPTER I

"... it was here, in early April when the temperature had begun to rise and the nights were no longer cool, that disaster overtook them. A small party of pilgrims from Hardwar, who had been offered hospitality for a night, brought cholera with them."

"Sita ... made a bundle of their few belonging, and taking him by the hand led him away from the horror and desolation of the camp. .. leaving the bodies to the mercy of the crows and the vultures."

Cholera was one of the most dreaded plagues in India, and it is still endemic there. It was not only very contagious but did its work with terrifying speed. Vultures are eaters of carrion and invaluable as disposers of the dead so it would have been vultures more than any other scavengers who would have have dealt with the devastation in Hilary's camp.

from CHAPTER I

RUINS IN THE COUNTRY OUTSIDE DELHI

"They were both very tired by the time the walls and domes and minarets of Delhi showed on the horizon, wraithlike in a dusty, golden evening. Sita had hoped to reach the city before dark . . . but the child was too tired and too sleepy to go further."

The open country is littered with ruins for miles around the two remaining cities of Delhi – Old Delhi and New Delhi. For there have been many Delhis built here. This picture shows a handful of these ruins – now submerged among the ever-growing modern suburbs and the western-style high-rise flats.

from CHAPTER II

"A troop of brown monkeys settled in the branches of the peepul tree."

Brown monkeys – the '*bander-log*' – are the common monkeys of India and you will find them everywhere. They are considered sacred because of the Monkey God, Hanuman and there are many monkey temples in India – one of them on the top of Jacko, the highest peak in Simla, in whose shadow I was born. I have a soft spot for these monkeys, because we had a pet one of our own for many years; she was given to me when she was only a week or so old – her mother had been killed in the jungle – and her name was Angelina Sugar-Peas, and we loved her dearly.

GATEWAY IN THE KUDSIA BAGH

"*. . . picking their way across the short stretch of open ground that separated the Kashmir Gate from the dark, friendly thickets of the Kudsia Bagh.*"

'*Bagh*' means garden, and this one, built by a Begum Kudsia, is no longer full of dark friendly thickets as it was when Ash and Sita hid there, or when my sister Bets and I were young and used to play in the bagh. In these days it has been tidied up and is full of open spaces. But all the children of Old Delhi still play there as they did in our day, and there are still many trees and two lovely ruins: the gateway to what must once have been the Begum's palace and a triple-domed mosque behind it. And when I last saw it, it was still full of squirrels, birds and butterflies.

The woman whose body Sita and Ash found lying among the bushes of the Kudsia Bagh would have been a Mrs. Fraser. Poor Mrs. Fraser was very stout, and she had hysterically resisted the efforts of her would-be rescuers to lower her over the wall of Delhi, near the Kashmir Gate, in order to escape the massacre of the Europeans that was going on nearby. Losing patience with her, the frantic helpers pushed her over and, having jumped themselves, attempted to carry her to safety, but owing to her weight and her continued (and understandable!) hysterics, they were unable to carry her further than the Kudsia Bagh, where they were forced to leave her. One of the Officers who had struggled to carry her noted in a subsequent account of his own escape that since she had been so badly injured in her fall, she would probably have died long before the mutineers found her — adding piously "God rest her soul".

". . . little lost villages where life pursued a slow, centuries-old course, and news from the outside world seldom penetrated."

There are countless little villages like this one scattered all over the countryside. Mud walls enclosing small courtyards and mud-built houses, a white-washed mosque – probably built by the local landowner – and the inevitable and essential village pond which not only provides all the water needed for drinking, cooking and cleaning, but where the cattle and goats are watered, clothes are washed and pots and pans scoured, and – in summer time – the villagers bathe. This picture was taken by my sister Bets (Betty).

from CHAPTER III

"But they were clear of the cantonment now and out in the open country."

This picture, like the previous one, was taken by Bets and might be almost anywhere in the plains of India or Pakistan. She took it sometime in the nineteen sixties, but if colour-photography had been invented over a hundred years ago it could easily have been taken then, for this is the India that does not change. Even today mile after mile of the countryside looks like this: enormous spaces, with, in the Punjab, a faint line along the northern horizon that is the snows of the Himalayas. Clumps of feathery pampas-grass, and men ploughing in the same manner that their forefathers have done for centuries – this is India; timeless and immemorial India.

from CHAPTER II

MOUNTAINS TO THE NORTH-WEST OF GULKOTE

"Always on clear days, they could see the snow peaks, and the sight of them was a constant reminder to Sita that time was running out and that the winter was coming. And then, in October, when the leaves were turning gold, they came to Gulkote."

In this picture, also taken in October, you can see the leaves turning gold and the snow-line beginning to creep down with the approach of winter. This is not, of course, Gulkote; since for obvious reasons Gulkote is an imaginary place. The photograph is one that I took in Gulmargin Kashmir, in the autumn of 1963 when I returned after a long absence to do some research before starting to write "The Far Pavilions." It shows the 'twin peaks' which were always known in Gulmag as Sunrise Peak and Sunset Peak because one caught the first rays of the rising sun and the other the last rays of the sunset. Bets and I had been picnicking, and the little whisps of smoke come from a fire that our pony-men had lit to brew tea for themselves, and which one of them is putting out before we leave.

from CHAPTER III

BAZAAR SCENE

"In all the talk in the bazaars and the gossip of the loitering, chattering crowds, there had been no word of the troubles that were shaking India, or any mention of mutineers or Sahib-log. Gulkote was only interested in its own affairs and the latest scandals of the palace.

I have no idea where this particular picture was taken; though from the clothing of the people it must have been somewhere very much further south than the Punjab, and far removed from my imaginary State of Gulkote. But, except from such details as dress and the woven baskets, all bazaars have a lot in common, and the one in Gulkote would have been just as colourful and just as crowded, cheerful and noisy. And equally afflicted by dust and flies and bad little bazaar boys, of whom Ash became one.

from CHAPTER III

HIS HIGHNESS THE YUVERAJ

". . . the Rajah's first wife, who had died in child-birth, had left her lord a son; Lalji, the beloved . . . apple of his father's eye and pride of all Gulkote."

This anonymous little prince will never grow up to be the ruler of his state, since Maharajahs and Rajas, Maharanis, Ranis and Yuverajs have all been swept away by the march of progress. But this is how they dressed for state occasions in the old days, and personally I feel sad that they have gone. Many were undoubtedly a burden and a curse to their people, wasting the revenues and oppressing the poor, but many others were adored by their subjects, and there is no denying that they were all, the bad as well as the good, a splendid splash of colour and glitter in an increasingly grey world. The heroic deeds performed by their ancestors have become part of the legends of the land, and will be told by Indian story-tellers for centuries to come – as anyone who has read Todd's "Rajasthan" will know.

from CHAPTER III

NAUTCH GIRL

"... *a troupe of dancing-girls entertained the guests ... among the dancers was the Kashmiri girl, Janoo. An alluring, golden-skinned, dark-eyed witch, as beautiful, and as predatory, as a black panther.*"

An Edwardian critic said of '*Nautch*-girls', dancing girls, that, although their dancing seemed to be irresistible to Indians, the majority of Europeans found it monotonous since it consisted of posturing and attitudes with a continual shuffling of the feet and an occasional whirl, and the girls themselves were so loaded with gaudy silks and jewels that it was enough to hamper any other movement of the limbs. But this description is not too accurate in many cases. As you can see from this photograph, they were often young and beautiful. Incidentally, the dancer in this picture would have come from South India, and not from Kashmir as Janoo did.

from CHAPTER III

"THE SNOWS AT DAWN"

"... *at its back the wrinkled, wooded foothills swept upwards to meet the white peaks of the Dur Khaima and the great snow-capped range that protects Gulkote from the north.*"

As I have already said, Gulkote exists only in my imagination. I built it up out of all sorts of bits and pieces of other princely states and cities and scenery that I remembered, and this picture is just one of those pieces. The Himalayan peaks shown here lie far to the south-east of Gulkote, for this is Kanchanjanga, as my mother painted it over a quarter of a century ago from Darjeeling.

from CHAPTER III

KODA DAD KHAN

*"Koda Dad Khan, the Mir Akhor – the Master of Horse . . . was a Pathan. There was nothing
that he did not know about horses, and it was said of him that he could speak their language and
even the wickedest and most intractable became docile when he spoke to it."*

This sketch of a Pathan was made by a Major E.Molyneux D.S.O. in 1898 and given to
me by a friend, Pam Powell, whose mother's first husband was Molyneux. The Major
evidently carried a sketch-book whenever he went on service in India during the last half
of the 19th century, and eventually became a painter of note. He illustrated Sir Francis
Younghusband's "Kashmir", a book that was first published in the early years of this
century – the same Younghusband who also wrote "*The Story of the Guides*" which I
found of great use when writing "*The Far Pavilions*". This is the only signed and dated
Molyneux sketch that I possess and the man he has drawn here is very like my idea of
Koda Dad Khan – two reasons why I am particularly fond of it.

from CHAPTER IV

A GARDEN IN THE HAWA MAHAL

*"A garden set about with walnut trees and fountains,
where a little pavilion reflected itself in a pool full of lily
pads and golden carp. At the far side of the garden only a
low stone parapet lay between the grass and a sheer drop of
two hundred feet onto the floor of the plateau below, while
on the other three sides rose the palace: tier upon tier of
carved and fretted wood and stone, where a hundred
windows looked down upon tree tops and city, and out
towards the far horizon".*

from CHAPTER IV

B Kaye and M.M. Kaye

THE WEDDING

"Lalji was married the following year and . . . all Gulkote enjoyed the spectacle and relished the gifts of food and money distributed to the poor."

This is a procession of women decked in their best and on their way to the Zenana quarters, where the bride will be being dressed for her wedding by her mother and sisters, friends and waiting women. A member of this procession is carrying gifts on a tray covered with a golden cloth. At a wedding that I attended many years ago I was presented with the cloth that had covered one such tray, and I have it still. The green silk of which it was made has not faded and the embroidery on it was obviously done in real gold thread, for it still shows no trace of tarnish. I doubt if real gold will ever again be used so lavishly, if at all, on a mere covering for a wedding present.

from CHAPTER IV

JULI

"She thrust out a thin, square little palm and the moonlight glinted on a small sliver of mother-of-pearl carved in the semblance of a fish. It was, Ash knew, the only thing she had to give: the sole trinket she possessed and her deaerest and greatest treasure. Seen in these terms it was perhaps the most lavish present that anyone could or would ever offer him, and he took it reluctantly, awed by the value of the gift."

from CHAPTER V

" . . . *A cluster of snow peaks that faced the Queen's balcony: a crown of pinnacles that lifted high above the distant ranges like the towers and turrets of some fabulous city, and that were known in Gulkote as the Dur Khaima – the Far Pavilions.*"

This is what the Queen's Balcony would have looked like on the night that Ash escaped from the Palace of the Winds. My sister painted it for me after reading the novel. India is full of such balconies, most of them built for the use of women in purdah, so that they could see without being seen. The balcony in the picture would originally have been entirely screened with pierced and carved marble, but as you see, the part facing the mountains has fallen out and only the pillars and pieces of side tracery remain.

This pencil sketch of a little Indian girl is one of my sister's drawings, and I think that the child 'Juli' must have looked very like this by the time Ash left Gulkote.

from CHAPTER IV

THE RIVER AT EVENING

"The river was bright with the sunset as he knelt on the wet sand and scooped up the water and drank greedily . . . there was nothing left in the shallow cave to show that anyone had ever been there . . . Nothing but the footmarks and a slight depression in the sand where Sita had lain."
"Ashton Hilary Akbar Pelham-Martyn shouldered his bundle and his burdens, and turning his back on the past, set out in the cold twilight to search for his own people."

This picture is a sketch done long ago, in the days of the Raj, by my mother. I have used it here because it seems to me to illustrate the scene I have described in Chapter 6 of "*The Far Pavilions*". It not only has the outcrop of rock that could well contain a shallow cave such as Sita and Ash sheltered in, but there are even footsteps in the sand, and distant hills. But, in fact, the river in the picture is not the Jhelum, but the Indus, and the hills are in tribal territory – the North West Frontier hills of what was then India, and is now Pakistan. But this is the river – 'the Father of Rivers' – that Ash had to cross to escape from the Punjab and reach Mardan.

from CHAPTER VI

THE PESHAWAR ROAD

" . . . *Ash took the road that leads from Attock to Peshawar.*"

My mother did this sketch many years ago. A party of Powindahs, a roving gypsy-like tribe from Afghanistan who are always on the move and who winter each year in Pakistan, were camping by the Peshawar road, and mother stopped and got out her paint-box and made a quick sketch of them with the tribal hills in the background.

from CHAPTER VII

MARDAN FORT

" . . . *the little star-shaped fort that Hodson built in the years before the Great Mutiny.*"

This is the fort that Hodson of Hodson's Horse built at Mardan in 1853-54, and except for the fact that the Guides, whose home was here for close on a hundred years, planted many trees in their cantonment so that nowadays the fort is surrounded by them, it is very much the same today as it was then.

"*Picture to yourself an immense plain, flat as a billiard table but not as green, with here and there a dotting of camel-thorn about eighteen inches high by way of vegetation. This, as far as the eye can see on the west and south of us, but on the north the everlasting snows of the mighty Himalayas above the lower range which is close to our camp.*"

"*Three weeks later Ash was in Bombay . . . en route to the land of his fathers*".

from CHAPTER X

PELHAM ABBAS

"Pelham Abbas the seat of Hilary's elder brother, Sir Matthew Pelham-Martyn Bart, was an imposing property consisting of a long square Queen Anne house, built on the site of the earlier Tudor one that had been destroyed by Cromwell's men in 1644 . . ."

This is the sort of house Pelham Abbas would have been. There would have been terraces and gardens at the back, as well as stables, greenhouses and walled kitchen gardens to the left and right. But to Ash, a child who had lived in an Indian palace where there would have been literally hundreds of rooms, a house such as this would have seemed dismally small and unimpressive.

from CHAPTER VII

BOMBAY HARBOUR 1872

"*The S.S. Canterbury Castle lay silent and apparently deserted in the mid-day heat.*"

This harbour was once one of the most beautiful in the world, and Kipling called Bombay 'the Queen of Cities.' He would not recognise her now. And neither do I, for concrete and high-rise buildings in the western mode have replaced the cool white bungalows, the shady gardens and the massed greenery of lonely Malabar Hill. Only the Parsee's 'Towers of Silence' still remain. But in the evening when the fishing boats sail out into the sunset and the dusk comes down, a little of the lost magic returns.

from CHAPTER IX

THE TRAIN JOURNEY

"*The Mail Train was not due to leave until the late evening.*"

This is the kind of train that Ash and Belinda, and their friends would have travelled in.
The carriages would have been very hot, dust would have leaked in through a hundred
cracks and crevices and the journey would have taken many days, since at that time
15 miles an hour would have been regarded as dangerously fast. It is often forgotten that
the British built a superb network of railways in the subcontinent which united countless
cities, towns and villages – and uncounted families, relatives and friends.

from CHAPTER I X

THE GHATS.

"The tree clad gorges . . . of the south . . ."

These are the ghats, through which the railway-line runs after leaving Bombay. They are still as beautiful as ever; and not too unlike this romantic picture that was "*Drawn on the spot in 1803 by William Westall, A.R.A.*" It is a pity that modern sightseers are generally in such a hurry that they prefer to fly rather than waste time going by train, since they miss a great deal by doing so.

from CHAPTER IX

THE JUMA MASJID, DELHI.

" . . . *the following morning, in company with Zarin, Ala Yar, Mahdoo and Gul Baz, he joined the
vast congregation in the courtyard of the Juma Masjid and said a prayer for Sita and for Uncle
Akbar – the one an orthodox Hindu and the other a devout Mussulman – in the belief that the one
God, to whom all creeds are one, would hear and not be offended.*"

The day would have been a Friday, which is the Mohammedan sabbath. And anyone
who visits the Juma Masjid today will see exactly the same sight as Ash and his
companions saw then.

from CHAPTER IX

THE KUTAB MINAR

" . . . George Garforth had taken advantage of Ash's absence to take them for a picnic to the Kutab Minar."

No one seems to be quite certain why this stupendous tower of fluted and carved red granite was built. Was it intended to be the minaret of some enormous mosque? Or a tower of Victory? Or a piece of showing off by Kutab-ud-din-Aibak, who began it in 1206, but did not live to see it finished? (That was done by his successor, who completed it in 1211). I myself prefer the story that I was told by one of the malis (gardeners) at the Kutab when I was a child. According to him, the king wished to marry a Hindu princess who refused him on the excuse that she had made a vow that she would say her prayers twice a day within sight of the sacred river Ganges. So he built this tower, from the top of which you can see for many miles, married the girl and made her climb it twice a day to say her prayers. I am afraid the mali's story is apocryphal, for I do not believe it would be possible to see the Ganges from there even with a powerful modern telescope and the clearest of clear days. But its a much nicer story than the others, isn't it?

from CHAPTER IX

THE GUIDE'S CAVALRY ON PATROL

"The Corps of Guides were back once more in their barracks after months of hard campaigning and harder fighting in the Yusafzai country . . ."

The Corps of Guides were kept on perpetual alert and expected to be able to leave on active service at a moment's notice. Their prestige was such that even their enemies applied to join them, and places in the Regiment were hotly competed for. In Kipling's famous poem 'The Ballad of East and West', that contains that often quoted line '*East is East and West is West, and never the twain shall meet*' the 'westerner' was an officer of the Guides.

from CHAPTER VII

CAMP SCENE

"November saw the beginning of squadron training, and Ash exchanged his hot, high room in the fort for a tent on the plains beyond the river."

In the Indian Army, Regimental Training was always a part of the cold weather, for during the hotter months the high temperatures made life under canvas as near intolerable as makes no matter. Though it had to be endured when on active service. Fortunately even the most hostile of tribes preferred to conduct the wars in the cooler weather whenever possible.

from CHAPTER XI

POINT TO POINT

"Ash rode over to deliver his Christmas presents at the Harlowe's bungalow and to enter his name for the Boxing Day Point-to-Point, which to Belinda's delight he subsequently won by a short head."

This picture is, of course, of a much later date than December 1871, when Ash rode in that point-to-point on the open country beyond Peshawar. It was taken about thirty years later, and comes out of an old photograph album that belonged to my father-in-law, who may have been one of the riders. But the country is either Peshawar or Quetta, and in either case, those are the Border hills in the background. And except for the shape of their pith hats, the clothes of the riders would not be much different from those that Ash and his contemporaries would have worn.

from CHAPTER XI

A BALLROOM SCENE

"Belinda . . . rewarded him with two waltzes and the supper dance at the Boxing Day Ball that night."

The ball would have been held in the Peshawar Club, which as far as I know is the same building – or part of the same building – that stands there still, and in which the residents and the garrison of Peshawar held so many balls in the days of the Raj – and still do. The North-West-Frontier Province is no longer a part of India but of Pakistan, and wine and spirits may no longer be drunk in the famous bar of the old Peshawar Club from which all women were rigorously excluded.

from CHAPTER XI

THE BRIDAL CAMP

"The assembly sent by the Maharaja of Karidkote to escort his sisters to their wedding outnumbered the citizens of Deenagunj by almost four to one, and Ash arrived to find the town a mere annex to the camp, the bazaar sold out of all foodstuffs and fodder and rapidly running short of water, the city fathers in a state of near hysteria and the District Officer, nominally in control of the camp, down with malaria."

from CHAPTER XIV

THE BRIDES' RUTH AND TROTTING-BULLOCKS

" . . . it had been expected that the brides would travel on elephants on the journey. But the slow, rolling stride of the great beasts made the howdahs sway, and the youngest bride . . . complained that it made her feel ill, and demanded that both she and her sister, from whom she refused to be parted, be transferred to a ruth – a bullock-drawn cart with a domed roof and embroidered curtains."

In India 'purdah women' of good family when going on visits or on pilgrimage, had to travel in covered vehicles so that they could not be seen. The richer ones frequently used this type of double – domed cart, harnessed to either one or two trotting bullocks. Anyone who has read Kipling's classic, 'Kim', will remember that the old lady whom Kim and the Lama met on the Grand Trunk Road was travelling in a ruth like this one.

from CHAPTER XIV

*"The uproar and confusion that would have conveyed, to an alien eye, an impression of riot aroused
no dismay in one who had been brought up in the bazaars of an Indian city."*

In a camp of this size there would of necessity be an enormous number of camp-followers:
women and children as well as men. Not to mention the pack-animals that would be
needed to carry baggage and pull carts full of grain and fodder and other supplies. Only
a very small section of the six thousand camp-followers that accompanied the Karidkote
Princesses would be able to cram themselves into this picture, but the ones who could
would have looked like this.

from CHAPTER XIV

M.M.Kaye

" *. . . a pile of cushions on which sat a plump, pallid little boy . . . and it occurred to Ash, bowing in*
acknowledgement to the boy's greeting . . . that it was a pity that all young princes should be so
plump, cross and frightened. Or at least, all the ones that he himself had met so far. Ash had seen
fear too often not to recognise it, and the signs were all there: the wide, overbright eyes and the swift
glances that flickered to the left and right and back over the shoulder . . ."

SIKH CAVALRY IN CAMP

"*The mile-long column moved at a foot's pace, plodding through the dust at the same leisurely pace as*
the elephants and stopping at frequent intervals to rest, talk or argue, to wait for stragglers or draw
water from the wayside wells."

This is an old print that appeared in '*Martins' Indian Empire*' a few years after the
Mutiny, and the Karidkote camp would have looked very much like this as they rested
under the shade of a banyan tree on the line of march.

from CHAPTER XIV

A JHEEL

"The mid-day meal was served in a large grove of trees near the edge of a jheel . . ."

A jheel is a large expanse of shallow water or, in some cases merely marshy ground, in
the fringes of which snipe can be found, and where large numbers of duck, teal and
geese, coot, herons and kingfishers and many other varieties of waterbirds congregate.
This sketch of a jheel was painted by an old lady of whom I was very fond – 'Lolly'
Maynard. She died a good many years ago, and her brother sent me a whole album of
her sketches, most of them made when she was a young bride in the years before the First
World War. I think she would have been delighted to know that some of her pictures
would one day appear in a book like this.

from CHAPTER XVI

THE DUST STORM

*"The sky ahead had been clear and calm, and even now the last of the sun lay gold along the crest of
the near hill. But as they turned they saw that behind them lay . . . a brown turgid curtain of
darkness that spanned the horizon from left to right and was advancing with such speed that it had
already blotted out the entrance to the valley."*

I have tried to show what a dust storm looked like to me. But it is impossible to convey
the awesome effect of that boiling, yellow-brown darkness. They can be frightening
things even when one is safe inside a house and able to shut every window and door
against them. And nothing can shut out the dust, which seems to be able to creep in
anywhere and everywhere, and takes days to get rid of when the storm is over. I can
only be grateful that I was never caught in one out in the open.

THE GOLCONDA TOMBS AT SUNSET

"The site chosen that day had been near a shallow expanse of weed-choked water that had evidently once been a man-made tank, dug many centuries ago to supply some long-forgotten city, traces of which still surrounded it."

The camp would not have seen these particular ruins, for the place where they stand lies much further south and is not a part of Rajputana. For these are the tombs of the Kings of Golconda – that fabled spot where diamonds were mined, and whose name stands to this day as a synonym for fabulous riches. I could not resist including it in this book, because whenever I look at it I can not only see India again, but smell the dusty scent of that evening in the plains when I watched my mother paint this picture of the tombs in the last of the sunset.

from CHAPTER XXII

SUNSET AND PALM TREES

"Each evening scouts rode on ahead to spy out the land and select the best available stopping place for the following day, and the tents were struck before first light . . ."

This sort of scenery would have become familiar to the camp as it moved towards Bhithor and the climate became dryer and hotter, for palms like these can grow in the most arid places as well as in damp and humid ones. I do not know where these particular ones grew, for this is another of dear Lolly's sketches – as is the one below – and neither of them carry a place-name or a date. But both are typical of much in India.

". . . he could see, not too far ahead a lone palm tree that rose above the waste of dusty ground and scattered grass clumps, and provided the landmark he needed."

"The diamonds in the tiny leaf glittered with a frosty brilliance and the great black pearl lay like a drop of glowing darkness on the white dust."

from CHAPTER XXII *and* CHAPTER XXVI

THE WALLS OF BHITHOR, A BHITHORI

"*. . . royal servants who, in accordance with a local custom wore the ends of their turbans wound about nose, mouth and chin in the manner of the veiled Tuaregs of the Sahara – an effect that was distinctly unnerving, in that it suggested footpads and violence.*"

"*The city had changed very little since the first Rana had built his capital in the region of Krishna Deva Reya. Its pale sandstone walls had an oddly bleached look, as though the burning suns of centuries had drained them of colour.*"

Bhithor, like Gulkote, lives only in my imagination, but I have taken a lot of details from other and real states in Rajputana. I am not sure where these particular walls come from – it looks to me like Gwalior, but it may be Bundi.

from CHAPTER XXVII

BHITHOR

"Bhithor was like something out of another age. An older and more dangerous age, full of menace and mystery. . . . the sharp-edged shadows were grey rather than blue or black, and . . . the blank and almost windowless faces of the houses gave Ash an uncomfortable feeling of claustrophobia."

This photograph of a street in Rajputana was taken by my mother, but so long ago that even she cannot be certain in which city she took it. But it is what I imagine Bhithor would have looked like.

THE RUNG MAHAL, BHITHOR

". . . at last they left the streets behind them, and dismounting in the entrance courtyard of the city palace the Rung Mahal, were conducted through a maze of dusty rooms and dark stone passageways to meet the Rana. Through here too there was the same claustrophobic atmosphere that had been so noticeable in the streets: the same stillness and stifling heat, the same haunting sense of an unforgotten past . . . of old times and old evil, and the unquiet ghosts of dead kings and murdered queens."

The 'Rung Mahal' means 'the Painted Palace' and as you see here the rooms of many Indian palaces were most beautifully painted with frescoes that time has faded to a softness that adds rather than detracts from their original, and possibly garish, splendour.

from CHAPTER XXVII

"By midnight the last of the long column marched out, leaving the cooking fires still burning, as Ash had given orders that the fires were to be left to die out untouched so that the watchers in the forts would be uncertain as to how many men had moved, and how many remained behind."

from CHAPTER XXIX

THE WEDDING

" . . . the state was aflutter with banners and garlands . . . tinsel and coloured paper and flowers. By the day of the wedding the very alleyways of Bhithor smelled of marigolds and jasmine instead of the more familiar mixture of dust and refuse and boiling ghee, while the hum of the city was drowned by the din of fu-fu bands and the crackle of patarkars."

These pictures show guests and gift-bearers arriving to attend a wedding. The silver salvers that are protected from the sun by embroidered cloths and by men carrying a canopy, contain presents for the bride. These may be special sweetmeats, fruit, nuts and cakes, or more valuable items such as jewellery or saris.

from CHAPTER XXIX

THE WEDDING

*"In an inner room of the Pearl Palace the brides were being bathed and annointed with scented oil,
the soles of their feet and the palms of their slender hands tinted with henna, their hair combed and
braided . . . Their women crowded about them, laughing and teasing and chattering like a flock of
gaily coloured parakeets as they dressed the brides in the shimmering silks and gauzes of their wedding
garments, painted their eyes with khol and hung them with jewels that were part of their dowries:
diamonds, emeralds, pigeon-blood rubies and ropes of pearls from the treasury of the Hawa Mahal."*

from CHAPTER XXX

" . . . one of the priests . . . began the lighting of the sacred fire. The flames illuminated his . . .
face as he leaned forward to feed the fire with chips of scented wood and grains of incense. When it
was well alight, silver platters heaped with perfumed salts were passed around to those who sat
within reach of the circle, each of whom took a pinch and threw it at the fire."

This photograph shows the sacred fire and the silver dishes that contain wood and incense
and perfumed salts with which to feed it, and one of the guests leaning forward to throw
a pinch onto the flames. The bride's face is hidden by her sari and her groom, who was
generous enough to allow this picture to be reproduced, asked that his features should
not be shown, he did not wish to be identified. So you cannot see the wonderful golden
headress that forms part of his turban, or the fabulous jewelled brooch that is pinned to it.

" . . . at nightfall the brides will leave for their husband's house."

CHAPTER XXX *and* CHAPTER XXXI

THE BRIDGE OF BOATS, ATTOCK

"Ash left his horse to be stabled and walked on down through the sleeping town, past the walls of the
Emperor Akbar's great stone fort that had guarded the ferry for close on two centuries.
The descendants of the first ferry-men still plied the trade of their forefathers, but they would soon
be gone, for the English had constructed a bridge of boats, over the Indus and nowadays nine tenths
of the traffic crossed by it."

The last time I crossed the Indus by the stone and iron bridge that replaced this one,
was in December 1963 and I was on my way back from Mardan. I had gone there – and
to Peshawer, Kohat and the Khyber – to research for *The Pavilions* and to get the feel of the
Frontier again. Attock looked just the same as I remember it in the days of the Raj – and
as it must have looked when Ash saw it. And I thought of all the Guides who have
passed through it on their way to and from Mardan during the years since the Corps
raised by Harry Lumsden moved into the fort that Hodson built for them on the plain
of Yusafzai. The Corps of Guides still flourishes, but their headquarters are no longer at
Mardan.

from CHAPTER XXXII

ON TREK

"Wally had joined him a day later and the two had trekked into Kashmir by way of Domel and the Jhelum Gorge."

In those days there was nothing that could be called a made road into Kashmir, and people on trek had to improvise their own where the track had been obliterated by a landslide. Here, in this photograph taken in the 1930s by Bill Magan, you can see what trekking in the Himalayas still involves.

from CHAPTER XXXII

A MOUNTAIN GORGE —KASHMIR

"... *through vast rock gorges and forests of pine and deodar ... and along tracks that were no more than narrow shelves scraped out of mountainsides that dropped sheer away to where the foam-torn Jhelum River roared in spate three hundred feet below.*"

Here you can see one of those tracks winding along a mountainside like a thread of cotton. And down there in the bottom of the valley is the river, looking, from this distance, like a tiny and innocent little stream. But if you were to climb down there, you would discover it to be a raging torrent, with huge logs being swept down with it to the plains. For the logging camps in the mountains use the river to take all that they cut down to the plains, and though some logs may take years to reach the end of the journey, nearly all eventually get through, since no log-jam can survive the torrents that pour through the narrow gorges when the snow melts on the high peaks and the river is in spate.

from CHAPTER XXVIII

DAL LAKE

"*. . . the Dal Lake was ablaze with lotus blossoms and alive with the flashing blue and gold and green of innumerable kingfishers and bee-eaters.*"

This is the last picture I painted in Kashmir before we left for England in 1947. India had just become independent and a brand new country, Pakistan, had been born. Goff and I, our packing done and our goodbyes said, left the children in Srinagar with my mother and took a last holiday in a houseboat on the Dal Lake. I painted several pictures in those few days, to keep as mementoes. And this one is the view from the roof of our boat, looking across Nasim Bagh to the takht-i-Suliman – the throne of Soloman – with its little stone temple on top and its far frieze of snows behind it, dark against the sunset. When I returned in the autumn of 1963, there were few changes: but sad to say, few lotus flowers either, since nowadays the village children pick the buds before they have time to open, and sell them to tourists for a few annas, so that a day may come when there are no more lotus on the Dal.
The takht which looked bare and rocky then is now covered with the trees that were planted to prevent erosion in the late nineteen thirties. And as many more trees have grown up in Nasim Bagh, you can no longer see the mosque that stands among them – Hazrat Bal, where there is a sacred relic; a hair from the beard of the Prophet. But I hope very much to see it all again soon. And not for the last time, either.

from CHAPTER XXXIII

"*Half way through July the weather broke, and after enduring three days of pouring rain and impenetrable mist on a mountain side, the campers beat a hasty retreat to Srinagar.*"

In the old days many officers of the Indian Army spent their 'local leave' shooting in and around Kashmir, and they would have had to go very high up to find such prized trophies as ibex and markor.

from CHAPTER XXXIII

". . . They bathed and lazed, gorged themselves on the cherries, peaches, mulberries and melons
for which the valley was famous, and visited Shalimar and Nishat – the enchanting pleasure-gardens
that the Mogul Emperor, Jehangir, son of the great Akbar, had built on the shores of the Dal."

This is a picture that I took of Hari Parbat Fort in the late evening. The sun had already
gone down behind the line of snows in the background, but the sunset sky was reflected
in the lake, and a little shikarra – the flat-bottomed wooden boats of Kashmir – was
being paddled past. I just caught it in time, and the picture is one that I treasure.
When Jehangir, who loved Kashmir, lay dying, they asked him if there was anything
he wanted, and he replied "Only Kashmir".
I can sympathise with him.

from CHAPTER XXXIII

ANCIENT TEMPLE AT HALWUD

*". . . exploring the countryside beyond the city, where the ground was littered with the relics of a
great past, now overgrown by creepers and almost forgotten: old tombs and the ruins of temples
and water tanks, built of stone that had been quarried in hills many miles to the north."*

This is another print from a book that Goff gave me for my birthday when we were
stationed in Chester, called *'Scenery Costumes and Architecture of Western India'* and published
in 1826. The pictures in it were mostly based on drawings and sketches made by a
Captain Grindlay during his service with the East India Company, and this one is of
an ancient temple in northern Kathiaway, which is part of the great peninsular of
Gujerat. Grindlay writes of "The splendid architectural remains in the city and environs
of Ahmedabad". But from what I hear, modern Ahmedabad is a vast industrial city,
and I suspect that many of these ruins, like those that used to surround New Delhi,
have been submerged in a forest of factories and high-rise flats. But if Hahdoo were to
return today, he would still be able to say his prayers on a Friday in the mosque in
Ahmedabad where Sultan Ahmed Shah, the founder of the city, lies buried.

from **CHAPTER XXXV**

THE LAKE AT MOUNT ABU

*". . . Gobind and Manilal, accompanied by Sarji's shikari, Bukta, who was to guide them to
Bhithor by way of Palanpore and the foothills below Mount Abu . . ."*

Another print from my book of old prints of Western India, and presumably based too
on a sketch by Captain Grindlay. My daughter Carolyn was born in Mount Abu, and
I used to take her in her pram for walks around this lake and past that little temple
that you see in the picture. She was born in the little military hospital in Mount Abu,
a lengthy and rather alarming proceeding that was enlivened by the fact that a tiger
killed the hospital's water-buffalo almost under my window. My doctor sat up for the
tiger a week or so later, in a nearby tree, and shot it. But not before it or one of its
relations had killed the sister-in-law of my dhobi (laundry man), who had been cutting
grass in the jungle. Since tigers are now an endangered species, I imagine that there
are no more of them in Mount Abu in these days: except that the famous Jain temples
are here, and the Jains are a sect who consider it is a sin to take the life of any living
thing, human or otherwise. Mount Abu is also the place where Sir Henry Lawrence's
wife, Honaria, died and was buried. The house that they lived in, and in which she died,
is still there. And her grave can be seen in the little cemetery.

from CHAPTER XXXVI

*"The spurs and ridges ran this way and that in an aimless, featureless maze. But Bukta appeared
to see and recognise landmarks that were invisible to his companions and he pressed ahead
unhesitatingly, riding where the ground permitted, and where it did not, plodding forward on foot,
leading his pony along narrow rock ledges or across precipitous slopes of shale or slippery,
sun-bleached grass."*

This is another photograph taken by Bill Magan, while on trek, and shows exactly
the sort of country that would have been crossed in order to reach my fictional state of
Bhithor.

from CHAPTER XXXIX

"The alleyway skirted that side of the Rung Mahal where the Zenana Quarter lay . . ."

This part of an Indian palace, and the curtained windows and fretted stone that screens the little windows that flank the upper balcony indicated that it is probably the Zenana Quarter where the purdah women live, secluded from the gaze of men. 'Purdah' means curtain, so to be 'in purdah' means to be 'behind the curtain'. The custom is not a Hindu one but was adopted from Mohammedan conquerors, and came to be almost universally used among the middle and upper class Indian women; and even among many – though by no means all – of their humbler sisters.

from CHAPTER XL

"The door of Gobind's house was barred, and anyone deputed to keep guard on it must have been swept up and carried along with the crowd minutes ago . . ."

This beautiful door with the sunlight glinting on the metal bosses with which it is studded, and the intricate stone carving that surrounds it, is an example of the skill, imagination and endless patience of Indian craftsmen. The little carved niche on either side would have held a chirag, one of the small earthenware lamps that are lit by the millions all over India to celebrate Diwali, the 'Feast of Lights', and also for weddings or other festive occasions. The ones here would have been lit every night for the convenience of visitors.

from CHAPTER XLI

A CHATTRI

" . . . The water was . . . green and stagnant and full of weeds, and many of the chattris were half ruined. Pigeons, parrots and owls had built nests in crevices between the stones and among the weathered carvings that decorated pediments, archways and domes . . . and the trees were full of birds quarrelling with each other as they come home to roost."

This photograph was taken by my sister towards evening, and is part of a chattri in Rajputana. It was falling in ruins, and as you can see, the roots of trees that years ago seeded themselves between the stones are helping to destroy it; but the fact that they are there adds to the romantic beauty of a building that will soon be lost, like the castle of the Sleeping Beauty, behind a screen of leaves and creeper.

from CHAPTER XL

A CHATTRI AT EVENING

"There were buildings everywhere. Memorial chattris. Vast, empty, symbolic tombs, built of the local sandstone and intricately and beautifully carved, some of them three and four storeys high so that their airy, domed pavilions . . . stood well above the tree tops. Each chattri commemorated a Rana of Bhithor, and had been raised on the spot where his body had been burned. And each, in the manner of a temple, had been built to surround or face onto a large tank, so that any who came to pray could perform the proper ablutions."

This particular chattri commemorates the Rajah of Bhurtpore who defeated all the attempts of the British, under the command of General Lake, to take his citadel. Lake's forces besieged it for months, and in the course of four assaults that were launched against it, lost more than 3,000 men. He never took Bhurtpore, but the Rajah, becoming bored by the whole affair, signed a truce with General Lake and promised to pay an indemnity of twenty lakhs of rupees. Whether he ever paid it, I don't know. But I do know that while taking this photograph of his chattri, I slipped and fell into the water, which was green and muddy and full of lethargic turtles and catfish. I had the presence of mind to fling the camera onto the shore, but I was soaked to the skin, and my host (the then Rajah) roared with laughter and said that his revered ancestor has never had much use for the British Army, and must have known that I was the wife of a British General and arranged to have me pushed in on purpose.

from CHAPTER XL

" . . . standing up in his stirrups he could just reach a first floor window . . . There was no light in the room behind it – or, as far as he could see, in any part of the house. But when he hammered on the lattice with the butt of his whip, Manilal's round, pale face appeared in the opening."

This window could only have been designed and carved in the east, and though I don't know where it is, it must be the window of a room in one of the many palaces in Rajasthan – the 'Country of Kings'. It's nice to imagine queens looking out of it in the old days to watch their lords come home from hunting or ride out to make war on a neighbouring king.

from CHAPTER XLI

THE CHATTRI

"*. . . was a larger and more elaborately decorated version of the far older one where he had left Dagobaz, being built in the form of a hollow square surrounding a vast tank . . . from the level of the terrace and facing inward, wide, shallow stone steps led down to the water's edge. The chattri had been built to face eastward into the sunrise and the clustered trees, but directly behind it lay the open ground, and today the western pavilions looked down onto a hastily constructed brick platform . . . where half-a-dozen priests were constructing a pyre from logs of cedar and sandlewood strewn with aromatic spices.*"

This is the chattri of another Rajah who evidently took a poor view of the British. If only I had had a better camera with me I would have taken a photograph of the charming frescoes that decorate the ceiling of the topmost pavilion and show opposing armies of Indians and British soldiers, their faces exactly alike and only the scarlet of the uniforms identifying the British who are all falling stiffly back in rows – shot dead by the Rajah's troops. It is a beautiful building, more like a palace than a tomb, and I used it for the chattri in my novel – adding one more pavilion to the tier you see in this picture.

from CHAPTER XLI

THE SUTTEE GATE

". . . the Suttee Gate with its pathetic frieze of red hand prints had always filled her with horror, and she could not bear to pass that tragic reminder of the scores of women who had made these marks – the wives and concubines who had been burned alive with the bodies of dead Rajahs . . . and who had dipped their palms in red dye and pressed them against the stone as they passed out through the Suttee Gate on their last short journey to the funeral pyre."

Suttee, the practice of voluntary immolation of a widow on the pyre of her dead husband, had been practised in India for centuries, and an early traveller in the country, Nicolo Conti, was told that between two and three thousand of the 12,000 wives of one of the kings, had been selected on condition that they would 'voluntarily' burn themselves on his death, which was considered a great honour. The British outlawed the practice of Suttee in 1830, but that did not mean that it stopped; and the last one to be publicly recorded – and by the press of half the world – took place not very long after the Raj ended, when the widow of a Sandhurst-trained Indian General insisted upon her right as a Hindu to burn herself on his pyre. This she did, to the tumultuous applause of an adoring crowd of thousands, having ordered her young son to set light to the pyre.

from CHAPTER L

As far as I can discover, the only Suttee Gates (and there are many) that still bear hand prints, are those where the hands have been carved to stand out in relief. Presumably because wind and weather have gradually worn away the stain, so that the marks were fading and would soon have been lost. I imagine that this is true, for the gates were not enclosed places that sun and rain and wind could not reach, and it stands to reason that by now very few of those little handprints can still be seen; and those few can be barely visible.

SHUSHILA

"Ash had not seen her at first. But a movement near him made him turn his head, and . . . he saw Shushila. Not the Shushila he had expected to see – bowed, weeping and half-crazed by terror, but a queen . . . a Rani of Bhithor. The small, brilliant figure was not only alone, but walking upright and unfalteringly, and there was pride and dignity in every line of her slender body."

from CHAPTER XLII

THE HATHI POL

"The few who had remained on guard at the palace were hastily rounded up and dispatched at full gallop to the Hathi Pol, the Elephant Gate, with instructions to cut off a party of five horsemen who were presumed to be making for the border."

The gate you see here is the Delhi Gate of the Red Fort in Delhi – though my sister and I always called it the Elephant Gate, and I suspect that most people think of it like that. This photograph came out of one of our family albums, and I imagine it was taken by my father, because that's mother on the left hand side, wearing a large brimmed sun-hat and – of all things – a lot of fur (it must have been January) with me sitting behind her, and Bets sitting opposite me on the other side of the gate: both of us wearing 'topis'.

from CHAPTER XLIII

"He watched Ash take out the service revolver and sight along the barrel, and said in an undertone: "It is all of forty paces. I have never handled one of these things. Will it reach as far?"

This is a central-fire army-issue revolver and would have been the kind that Ash would have carried.

from CHAPTER XLII

". . . they found the cargo-boat Morala at anchor, and went on board to collogue with her owner, Captain Red Stiggins."

These are fishing boats, and not the kind that the *Morala* would have been, since she was a coastal trading boat, built to carry cargo to various ports in India and Arabia. The *Morala* would therefore have been a good bit bigger, though she too could have used sail, for steam was still in its infancy and only large passenger ships or Navy ships made use of it. But the boats you see here can still be seen in almost any port east of Suez, and very picturesque they look when under sail, or riding at anchor as in this picture. Red would have recognised them – and so would Ash.

from CHAPTER XXXV

ON THE INDUS

"A dundhi, a flat bottomed boat normally used for carrying cargo . . . had taken them up the Indus, initially under sail, and later, if the wind failed, by means of a tow rope. Teams of coolies had pulled the clumsy craft from village to village, a fresh team taking over each evening while the previous one turned homeward. [Their] tiny ramshackle cabin with its . . . matting walls might be exceedingly hot and far from comfortable . . . but the women's quarters in the Rung Mahal had been far hotter, while here the matting could be rolled up at will – and there outside lay the river and its white sandbanks."

The dundhis still ply their trade on the Indus, and as you see, the matting walls of their make-shift cabins can still be let down or rolled up at will. This photograph was taken in the nineteen-thirties by my mother, during a trip on the Indus, and this is the boat she travelled in. It too was either towed by teams of coolies when moving up-stream, or taken down by the current, guided by that huge wooden rudder. It was while on this trip that she painted *The River at Evening* reproduced earlier – the rocks and the river, the footsteps in the sand, and the sun setting behind the border hills.

from CHAPTER XLVIII

*"But with the Salt Range closing in to hem the river between high banks and shut out the breeze,
even the nights were no longer cool, while the days had become so hot that the cliffs of rock salt and the
blinding white sand by the water's edge, the ground underfoot and even the planks of the boat felt as
though they had come fresh-baked from a furnace."*

I don't know where this picture was taken, but I think it is beautiful, and it might well
be on the Indus where the Ranges close in and the river begins to narrow before it reaches the
great rock gorges below Attock. I remember how horrified I was when I was brought
home from India as a child and first saw an English beach. I could not believe that this
nasty biscuit coloured stuff was sand, because the only sand I knew was silver – like the
sandbanks of the Indus or the Ganges, or any of the great rivers of the Punjab. Even now
I still think of sand as silver – despite Shakespeare, and the fact that I live in Sussex by
the sea!

from CHAPTER XLVIII

WIGRAM BATTYE

"So Wally had talked, and Ash learned that the Guides were in 'tremendous shape' the Commandant and the other officers 'the best of fellows', and Wigram Battye in particular an 'absolute corker.' In fact the words 'Wigram says' recurred with such frequency that Ash was conscious of a fleeting twinge of jealousy."

Wigram Battye was one of three brothers who served in the Corps of Guides. The eldest, Quentin, died in 1857, the year of the Mutiny. He was killed at Delhi and lies buried there. Wigram and his younger brother Fred, both of whom were also killed in action leading the Guides into battle, are buried side by side in the old cemetery in Mardan, where I saw their graves in 1963. Their nephew, Ivan, followed his uncles into the Corps in 1895, and retired as Brigadier Battye, C.B., D.S.O., having been Commandant of the Guides Infantry from 1921 to 1925. This little picture of Wigram was drawn by my sister from a photograph of him.

from CHAPTER XLIX

BRITISH AND INDIAN OFFICERS OF THE GUIDES

Here you see a mixture of officers, obviously taken on active service by a 'reporting'
photographer attached to the Army. Newspaper correspondents would accompany the
army, though not in anything like the numbers that would do so today (so far, I have
only come across the reports of one; the Times correspondent). But I do not imagine that
there would have been many photographers, since at that time the process was still a
very slow one, and a correspondent would telegraph a report to England (that too would
take a fairly long time), and his newspaper's tame artist would draw a picture, based on
the report, which would be published instead of a photograph. Among those present in
this group you can recognise a few who appeared in the one on the opposite page. In
particular the 'O.M.', this time wearing a helmet, Hughes, without the little pill-box he
is wearing in the other photograph, Cooke-Collis who appears to have put on a lot of
weight, Stewart, Campbell and Hammond, and Fred, minus his helmet, sitting below
Stewart and between three of the Indian officers. A less flossy picture than the sedate one
taken (presumably) at Mardan a few months earlier.

GUIDES OFFICERS

This is a group photograph of Guides Officers taken in 1878, just before the outbreak of the Second Afghan War. That is Wally Hamilton striking a pose on the extreme right – and looking every one of his twenty-two years! Next to him sits 'Rosie' – Surgeon Ambrose Kelly – with Wigram's brother Fred standing between him and Stewart. Cooke-Collis stands between Stewart and 'Chips' Campbell, and next to Chips stands the 'O.M.', the 'Old Man' – Colonel Jenkins, the Commandant – with Hammond sitting on his right, then Hughes standing, and Wigram Battye seated at the far side of the group from Wally. What looks like a Guides waist-sash seems to have been spread at their feet – it looks too big to be a pugree (turban) cloth such as you see swathed round the helmets, but the stripes on it appear to be the same.

"he came out onto the verandah, and subsiding into a long-sleeve chair, gave himself up to thought."

This man, who except for the fact that he has no beard, could easily be Wigram, comes out of a book called 'Lays of Ind', written in the eighteen-seventies by someone who called himself "Aliph Cheem". It could also be the verandah of any bungalow from Peshawer to Madras, for chairs such as this, and the split-cane chiks that can be let down to keep out the sun or rolled up to let in the cooler air of evening, were common to most bungalows right up to the end of the Raj. And are probably still used to the present day.

from CHAPTER XL IX

VIEW FROM JAMRUD

"The five men had left Jamrud in the chill pre-dawn darkness, and as unobtrusively as possible. The moon was down and the stars were already fading, but in the east the sky was beginning to pale, and there was just enough light for the riders to be able to take their horses at a cautious trot across the stretch of plain that lay between Jamrud and the hills."

Jamrud, which is pronounced 'Jum-rood' and not, as you would expect, 'Jam-rud' is an old Sikh Fortress that was built to guard the mouth of the Khyber Pass in the days when the Sikh empire stretched from the Punjab to the hills of the Northwest Frontier.

from CHAPTER LII

"Once safely across the open ground and among the foothills they had dismounted, and leaving their horses in charge of the sowars, gone forward on foot. It had been a long and arduous climb, and the darkness had not helped, but as the sky overhead was beginning to lighten, they reached the summit . . . subsided thankfully on the ground and stared about them."

Sarkai Hill overlooks the Khyber Pass and the tribal lands that lie beside and beyond it, and this old photograph shows the Khyber side of the hill and 3 Guides officers with a small escort of sowars reconnoitering the Pass. Cavagnari and his party would have climbed this hill to spy out the land, after riding out from Jamrud.

from CHAPTER LII

THE KHYBER PASS AND ALI MASJID

"They were looking out across tribal territory: the secret and jealously guarded lands of men who recognised no law other than their own desires, and whose forefathers have for centuries swept down from those hills like wolf packs, to rob and lay waste the villages on the plains whenever the fancy took them. Something glinted brightly in the blaze of the rising sun; pinpointing an insignificant hill-top that until then had been indistinguishable among a hundred others. 'Guns', breathed Colonel Jenkins. 'Yes, that's Ali Masjid all right."

This picture of the Khyber Pass was painted in about 1847 by J. Rattray, and a lithograph was made from it by W. L. Walton. Like the vast majority of Victorian painters who made sketches in the East, Rattray has produced a romanticised picture of the Khyber, and I hate to tell you that Ali Masjid looks nothing like the Christmas-pudding shaped hill that you see pictured here. It is far less obtrusive and but for its fortress, barely distinguishable from the surrounding hills. But then I imagine that Mr. Rattray did not take too long over his sketch, but scribbled it down in haste for fear of being picked off by a bullet from a tribesman's jezail if he lingered too long. The tribes never took kindly to strangers, and had a particular dislike of map-makers and surveyors and other people who draw pictures. Nor are they very keen on photographers to this day.

from CHAPTER LII

This picture has always been a favourite of mine, and any Frontier Force officer will tell you that the artist has got every last detail right. When you look at it, you realise the enormous difficulty that faced any invading army advancing into this sort of territory, where every rock, stone, crevice or cranny could conceal an enemy sniper. And an enemy, moreover, who was familiar with every yard of his native hill and was an expert at laying ambushes.

From a painting by
V. M. Hamilton

JALALABAD

"Ash did not think that he would have much difficulty in arranging a meeting with Cavagnari once he reached Jalalabad. But he had not allowed for snow, and now he wondered if he would be able to get to Jalalabad at all . . ."

This drawing of Jalalabad was made during the first Afghan War. It would not have looked very different in the time of the Second Afghan War, when another British force occupied the city. But I doubt if anyone would recognise it today.

from CHAPTER LIII

JALALABAD BAZAAR

". . . the Shinwari had made his way to a small house in a backwater of the city where he was presently joined by a Risaldar of the Guides Cavalry, wearing civilian dress."

This photograph was taken during the occupation of Jalalabad in the Second Afghan War and shows part of the bazaar through which Ash and Zarin would have walked, and where Ash would have found lodging. A large part of the bazaar was covered, and you can see the beginning of the covered part in this picture, where the open street ends.

from CHAPTER LIV

KABUL RIVER ABOVE JALALABAD
'Ford O' Kabul River'

"The moon was still up when the two squadrons of Hussars and Lancers left camp, but it was sinking fast, and by the time the ford was reached it had been lost to sight behind the near hills, and the valley lay deep in shadow."

This is an old photograph, taken at the time of the 2nd Afghan War, of the Kabul River, not far from the ford above Jalalabad where 46 men of a single squadron of the 10th Hussars were drowned on an April night in 1879 while attempting to cross the river. The drawing shows a trooper of the 10th. Kipling wrote a poem about this tragic incident: 'Ford o' Kabul River', which was later set to music and has a most haunting tune. It is the lament of a trooper for his best friend who was drowned at the ford, and you will find it in 'Barrack Room Ballads'.

from CHAPTER LIV

BENGAL LANCERS

"The valley reverberated with the voice of the swollen river, and as the squadrons formed up in half sections, even the clash and jingle of accoutrements and the clatter of chargers' hooves could barely be heard above the roar of the rapids. But the local guide stepped confidently into the water and waded across, followed by the Bengal Lancers whose men, accustomed from childhood to the treacherous Indian rivers, had reached the far side in safety."

As this group photograph of the Bengal Lancers was taken in 1879, it is more than likely that some of the men in this picture were among those who crossed the ford ahead of the 10th Hussars, and reached the far bank in safety. There can be few people who have not heard of the Bengal Lancers, if for no other reason, because of the success of Yeats-Brown's book 'Bengal Lancer', and the film that was based upon it: 'Lives of a Bengal Lancer', starring the late Gary Cooper. A film that was an enormous box office success, and had the entire Indian Army in stitches. Their shouts of mirth must have been audible from Bombay to Boston, and I don't think poor Colonel Henslowe, who was the 'technical adviser' on that film, ever lived it down.

from CHAPTER LIV

"The guns fired again . . . And as the sound died, Wigram's right arm jerked upward, and from the waiting lines behind him came the answering rasp and glitter of steel as his two hundred men drew their sabres. He barked a command, and with a deafening cheer the cavalry charged –"

This is a squadron of Indian Cavalry charging. The officer, and his bugler who is sounding the charge, out in front, and the squadron racing knee to knee behind them. This is how the Guides would have looked to the enemy as they charged at Fatehabad though in fact this is a practice charge and the regiment is not the Guides, who would not have been carrying lances as only the Headquarter Company carried those. This is a squadron of the 3rd Cavalry which my future father-in-law was commanding at the time this photograph was taken, possibly about 1920.

from CHAPTER LV

"On the word his waiting gunners sprang to life and plying whip and spur, swept forward at a gallop, the gun-wheels bounding over the stony ground and the dust whirling up behind them. They raced on for five hundred yards, and then, pulling up, unlimbered the guns and opened fire at extreme range on the serried masses of the enemy on the heights."

This is the kind of field gun that the Artillery would have used at Fatehabad, and below it is a jezail – the long barrelled musket of the Frontier tribes – and a Cavalry-carbine such as the Guides would have carried. Contrasting these weapons, one is reminded of that cynical little rhyme from the hey-day of Colonial Empire — 'They may be right. But we have got the Maxim gun, and they have not.'

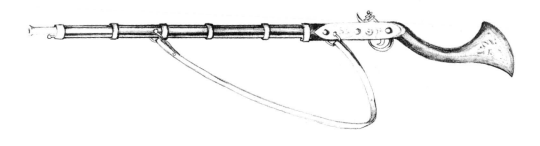

Drawings by M M Kaye

from CHAPTER LV

THE BATTLE OF FATEHABAD

"... *Wally reined in savagely, his face suddenly white. 'What the hell are you stopping for ',*
blazed Wigram furiously, struggling to rise. 'I'm all right. I'll come on directly Take 'em on
Walter! Don't mind me. Take 'em on boy'.
Wally did not pause to argue. He turned in the saddle, and shouting to the squadrons to follow him,
flourished his sabre about his head, and with a wild Irish yell spurred forward up the slope towards
the waiting enemy, the Guides thundering at his heels and shouting as they rode."

I found this picture in a book I bought at an auction for a few pence. The artist
presumably drew this picture from accounts he had read of the battle twenty-two years
earlier, and this is his idea of how it might have looked. The man with the beard is
obviously Wigram, whose horse has just been hit and is about to come down, and I
suppose the officer on the grey is meant to be Wally – though it is on record that Wally's
charger was called 'Mushki' which means 'the brown one'. There is a third British
officer on Wigram's left, but in fact there were only two British officers with the Guides
that day; Wally and Wigram. Nevertheless, it makes a nice illustration of a cavalry
engagement in the days of the Raj, so I will not quibble over details!

from CHAPTER LV

RESSAIDAR MAHMOUD KHAN,
Q.V.O CORPS of GUIDES
Killed in Action against the Khugianis
2nd April 1879

MAHMOUD KHAN

"Wally caught a glimpse of Zarin, teeth clenched in a ferocious grin as he drove the point of his sabre into the throat of a shrieking ghazi, and of Risaidar Mahmud Khan – his right arm hanging useless and his sabre gone, holding his carbine left-handed and wielding it like a club".

This picture, the original of which is still in the possession of the Guides, was painted in Jalalabad in 1879, and I made this copy of it for Goff. As the Risaidar was killed during the battle of Fatehabad – 'in personal combat with one of the enemy, whom he slew,' as it says in the 'History of the Guides' – the painting must have been done not long before he died. I would have liked to reproduce it in colour, but that was not possible. Goff has an Afghan knife that is the double of the one you see stuck into Mahmud Khan's waist belt.

from CHAPTER LV

JULI IN DISGUISE

"The Begum had provided Afghan dress for Aujuli, and charged Gulbaz with procuring two broken down nags in the bazaar, capable of bearing them, but unlikely to attract the attention or envy of even the most acquisitive tribesmen. She had herself stayed up to see them depart unobtrusively and by night, and as she bolted the little side gate behind them she sighed, remembering her own youth . . . 'Yes, I too would have done the same,' mused the Begum. I will pray that she will be permitted to reach Kabul in safety and find her man there."

This is how I think Juli would have looked wearing Afghan dress, on the journey to Kabul. The woman in the photograph is probably a Powindah – you can see the laden camel behind her – and they are, as I have said somewhere else in this book, gypsy-folk and very easy to talk to. The woman here has started to hide her face from the camera and then laughed and has changed her mind. I don't know who took this photograph or where. I found it among a lot of my mother's and she says she can't remember if she took it or not, but thinks it may have been taken on the road that crosses the Kohat Pass, much of which runs through tribal territory. Or perhaps in the Khyber itself?

from CHAPTER LIII

THE KABUL RIVER, RUNNING THROUGH THE GORGES

"*. . . in the dark hour before dawn the raft set out on the long and hazardous voyage to the plains . . . through the gorges where the Kabul River carves its way through the wild mountain country north of the Khyber, past Dakka and Lalpara and the whirlpools of the unknown Mallagori country.*"

This photograph shows part of those gorges, and even in so small a picture you can see how the river whirls through them, and how difficult it must have been to take a raft down them. The country is still as desolate as it was in those days and in 1938, when this picture was taken by Pat Macnamara of the Guides.

from CHAPTER LVI

"Daylight was beginning to fade when the look-out, who had lain all day on a ledge of cliff above the river, lifted his head and whistled in imitation of a kite. Sixty yards away a second man, concealed by a crevice in the rock face passed on the signal, and heard it repeated by a third. There were more than a dozen watchers lying in wait along the left bank of the gorge, but even a man with binoculars would not have suspected it, and the men on the raft had no such aids."

The tale of the journey of the raft down the Kabul River and the ambush that was laid for it, like much in "*The Far Pavilions*", is true. Which to my mind makes it far more exciting. I don't think I could have invented anything like that – or the incident of the stolen carbines either. There were so many true stories to choose from that the only difficulty was which ones to keep, and which ones to reluctantly discard – or perhaps keep for another day? Even the Guides seem to have forgotten this one, for it doesn't appear in either the 'History of the Guides' or Younghusbands 'Story of the Guides'. I found an account of it, cut out of an old copy of 'Blackwoods Magazine', among a box of letters and papers belonging to my husband's family, and I checked the story when I returned to the Frontier in 1963, and found that it was true.

from CHAPTER LVII

M. M. Kaye

THE MAGPIE

"You won't tell my wife we saw a magpie, will you? She wouldn't like it. She's always been superstitious about such things, and she'd think it was a bad omen and worry about it."

This is yet another true story. General Sir Frederick Roberts ,V.C., who became Field Marshall Lord Roberts of Kandahar, tells it in his autobiography 'Forty-One Years in India', which he published in 1897. As I myself always salute a magpie (and generally count ten backwards as well, just to be on the safe side) I naturally could not resist using it. And I am not the only one, because I discovered, when researching for *"The Far Pavilions"*, that Roberts must either have told that story to a great many people at that time, or else everyone who wrote about the 2nd Afghan War consulted him or read his book, for the tale of the magpie appeared again and again. But I still like it. Its the sort of trivial piece of real life that makes the past suddenly come alive.

from CHAPTER LIX

THE BALA HISSAR

*"The size of the Mission had been a disappointment to Wally, who had visualised a far larger and
more imposing cavalcade: one that would impress the Afghans and do credit to the British Empire.
The meagreness of the Envoy's party struck him as a depressing example of Government cheese-paring."*

This is the sort of country the Mission would have passed through on their way to Kabul.
Small Afghan villages with rather ramshackle looking buildings, and always among hills.

from CHAPTER LIX

THE BALA HISSAR

"The ancient citadel of the Amirs of Afghanistan was . . . surrounded by a long rambling outer wall, some thirty feet high and pierced by four main gateways . . . within this were other walls that enclosed the Amir's palace."

This old print of the Bala Hissar must have been done from a sketch made during the British occupation of Kabul at the time of the First Afghan War. We found it in the National Army Museum, and it is one of the most attractive drawings of the fortress that I have yet seen. By the time of the 2nd Afghan War, the Bala Hissar was looking a lot shabbier. Or else the artist who drew this picture was flattering his sitter in the manner of artists everywhere?

from CHAPTER LX

THE SHAH SHAHIE GATE

*". . . he had purposely stayed away, contenting himself instead with listening from the rooftop of
Sirdar Nakshband's house to the crash of bands and the boom of guns that heralded the Envoy's
arrival at the Shah Shahie Gate of Kabul's great citadel, the Bala Hissar."*

I drew this picture of the Shah Shahie Gate from various photographs of it, most of
which were taken later. This is how I think it would have looked on the day of the
British Mission's arrival. The great bazaar at Kabul was once roofed in, but it was burnt
by General Pollack in reprisal for the population's resistance when the city was captured
in the First Afghan War. This is how it must have looked when Cavagnari and his escort
of Guides came to Kabul.

from CHAPTER LX

KABUL BAZAAR

"... *he would go into the city and listen to the talk in the great bazaar, and discover what was being
said in the coffee shops and serais . . . and listen to the opinions of the citizens and men who were
passing through Kabul. Merchants with caravans from Balkh, Herat and Bakhara, peasants from
outlying villages bringing goods to market, Russian agents and other spies, soldiers drifting back from
the fighting in the Kurram or the Khyber, slant-eyed Turkomans from the north and men on
pilgrimage to one of the city's mosques.*"

from CHAPTER LVI

"In the course of the past few years, Wigram had seen a good deal of Wally's kinsman the Deputy Commissioner of Peshawer . . . Pierre Louis Napoleon Cavagnari was a curious person to be found occupying such a position, for . . . his father had been a French count who had served under the great Napoleon, become Military Secretary to Jerome Bonaparte, King of Westphalia, and married an Irish lady, Elizabeth, daughter of Dean Stewart Blacker of Carrickblacker [though despite his Gallic names the Deputy Commissioner, having been brought up in Ireland, had always regarded himself as British, and preferred his friends to call him 'Louis' because it seemed to him the least foreign of his three given names."

"The Amir had received the British Envoy and his suite with flattering cordiality and every sign of friendship."

Here in this carefully posed picture you see Sir Louis Cavagnari and his secretary, William Kenkyns, with the Amir of Afghanistan, Yakub Khan, his commander-in-chief, Daud Shah, and a member of his suite, Habibullah Monstifi, seated in the shade of a decorated tent. Sir Louis and William are wearing the full dress of Political Officers, and the Amir is a mass of gold lace and decorated in the western style, and not looking too happy.

from CHAPTER L *and* CHAPTER LX

BARBUR'S TOMB

" The last resting place of Barbur – 'Barbur the Tiger', who had seized the Land of Cain only a few
years after Columbus discovered America, and gone on to conquer India and establish an imperial
dynasty that had lasted into Ash's own lifetime – was in a walled garden on the slope of a hill to the
south west of the Shere Dawaza. The spot had been known in Barbur's day as 'The Place of
Footsteps', and it had been a favourite haunt of his."

Judging from this and other nineteenth century photographs of Barbur's tomb and the
garden in which it stands, it had been allowed to get sadly delapidated, and this was
how Ash and Wally would have seen it on Wally's 23rd birthday. But it was obviously
repaired and tidied up in the twentieth century, for I have seen recent pictures of it in
which are not in the least like this one. It's nice to know that 'The Place of Footsteps' is
now being properly cared for.

from CHAPTER LXI

"So that's why you were dressed up like a scarecrow and carried off the prizes for the opposition that day . . ."

"Ash had the grace to look ashamed of himself and say defendingly 'I hoped it might even up the balance a bit and take some of the heat out of the situation. But I didn't think you'd recognise me'. 'Not recognise you? When I know every trick of riding you possess and the way you always – Holy Smoke!'. It's yourself who's mad, so it is."

from CHAPTER LXI

" The lower Bala Hissar was a town in itself, crammed with the houses of courtiers and officials and all those who worked for them, and possessing its own shops and bazaars. It was in this part of the citadel that the Residency stood."

from CHAPTER LX

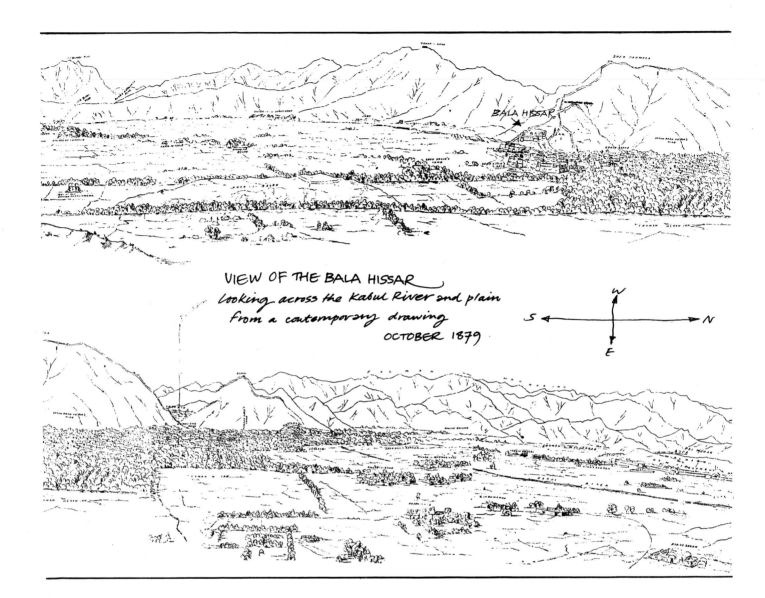

VIEW OF THE BALA HISSAR
Looking across the Kabul River and plain
from a contemporary drawing
OCTOBER 1879

THE SOUTH SIDE OF THE BALA HISSAR

"The citadel was built upon the steep slopes of a fortified hill, the Shere Dawaza, that dominated the city and a large part of Kabul. The whole Shere Dawaza hill was ringed by a wall that climbed the steep flanks and followed the line of rocky heights so that sentries manning the blockhouses here could look out at the enormous circle of mountain ranges, and down on palace and city, the entire sweep of the valley and the wide, winding ribbon of silver that was the Kabul River."

No foreigner has been allowed to go near the Bala Hissar for many years, and people who have visited Kabul quite recently have told me that they never even had a glimpse of it – in fact they did not even seem to know about it, or where it was, and it is easy to see why. Modern Kabul is so vast a place, and so many huge modern buildings have sprung up, that even the once great citadel must be difficult to see, with so much in the way. But there are still earthquakes, I hear. The only thing that stays the same through the centuries are the high snows that can be seen from anywhere in the valley.

from CHAPTER LX

'Look, we've got to get those guns. We've got to. I don't mean spike them. I mean capture them. If we can only get 'em back here we can blow the Arsenal sky-high. We've only got to land one shell fair and square on it, and all the ammunition and gunpowder inside is going to go up with a bang that will wreck everything within a radius of several hundred yards.''

This is the type of gun that the Afghans dragged into the Residency compound to use against the Guides entrenched in the barrack block. The guns would have been of an older and heavier design than the ones used by the British Artillery at Fatehabad, and were probably part of a consignment of arms given to the late Amir, Shere Ali, by a previous Viceroy, as a good-will gift from the Government of India.

from CHAPTER XLVII

FIGHT FOR THE RESIDENCY

"When the flimsy wood began to splinter and the rusty iron hinges bent and cracked they rushed to put their shoulders to the door, pushing against the rioters outside, but it was a losing game. As the last hinge snapped the door fell in on them and the crowd burst into the courtyard, and simultaneously, from somewhere outside, a shot rang out."

This is a newspaper artist's impression of the fight for the Residency, based on accounts that would have been sent home by telegraph from Simla. It was published in the 'Illustrated London News' in the autumn of 1879, and depicts Wally and the Guides fighting in the gateway of the Residency courtyard.

from CHAPTER XLIV

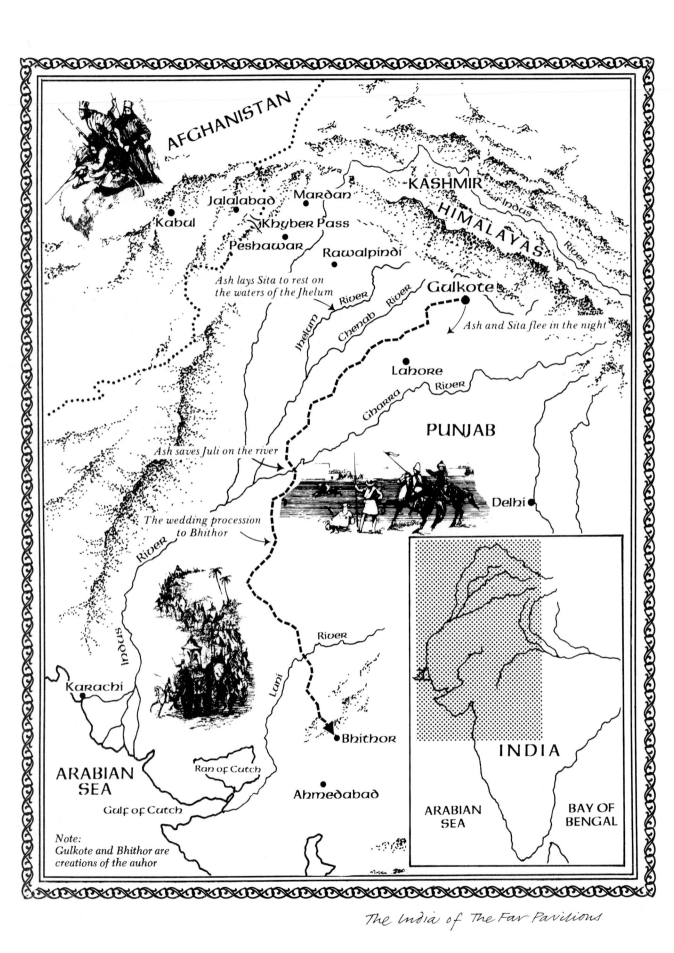

AFGHANISTAN

KASHMIR

HIMALAYAS

Indus River

Jalalabad

Mardan

Kabul

Khyber Pass

Peshawar

Rawalpindi

Gulkote

Ash lays Sita to rest on the waters of the Jhelum

Jhelum River

Chenab River

Ash and Sita flee in the night

Lahore

Gharra River

PUNJAB

Ash saves Juli on the river

Delhi

The wedding procession to Bhithor

River

Indus River

Karachi

River

Luni River

Bhithor

ARABIAN SEA

Ran of Cutch

Ahmedabad

Gulf of Cutch

INDIA

ARABIAN SEA

BAY OF BENGAL

*Note:
Gulkote and Bhithor are creations of the auhor*

The India of The Far Pavilions

THE MOUNTAINS AROUND KABUL AT SUNSET

"But now of a sudden it was as though he saw Kabul and its setting for the first time; not stark and desolate and dim-coloured, but beautiful with a wild, spectacular beauty that took his breath away. A combination of sunset and dust and the smoke of cooking fires had transformed the valley into a sea of gold, out of which the near hills and the jagged snow-capped ranges behind them rose up in layers after layer of glittering splendour, caught in the bonfire blaze of the dying day and flaming like Sheba's jewels against an opal sky. The soaring pinnacles of the mountains might have been the spires and towers of some fabulous city – Valhalla, perhaps; or the outer ramparts of Paradise."

This is an impression of the mountains of the Hindu Kush, seen from the valley of Kabul. The valley is ringed about with snow peaks, which are sufficiently spectacular at all times of day, but particularly at sunset. Any sunset among mountains anywhere in the world is always a marvellous sight, but never more so than in the Himalayas, the Hindu Kush or the Pir Panjal, for the dust of the plains and the smoke of cooking fires that, except after rain, seem to hang in the air even in high places, produces a depth of colour that is seldom seen elsewhere. The only trouble is that you can never get it onto paper quickly enough, for nothing fades so swiftly, and before one is half finished, the sunset has gone.

from CHAPTER LXIII

THE HANGU ROAD

"For the past twenty years he [Cavagnari] had served with distinction in India's Border lands [and] acquiring an enviable reputation for being able to manage the turbulent tribesmen, whose dialects he spoke with idiomatic fluency."

Cavagnari, and all Frontier Force Officers, both political or military, would have known this view well, for you can see the oddly shaped hill with its sharp shadows on the road to Hungu and the Kurram Valley. This part of the country lies in Tribal Territory, and this sketch comes out of one of the albums that we have always kept, and which include, in addition to photographs, all sorts of kinds of souvenirs of the places we have visited or lived in. I did this picture while we were on our way to Thal, a small fort that was a British outpost of Empire in the Kurram Valley in those days. You were not allowed to travel on this road without an armed escort, and our escort sat by the roadside and smoked bazaar cigarettes and gossiped while I painted and Goff went to sleep in the sun with his pith-helmet over his eyes.

from CHAPTER L

KOHAT PICKET. THAL, IN THE KURRAM

*"It did not strike him as odd that Cavagnari proposed to travel to Kabul by way of the Kurram
Valley rather than by the far shorter and easier route through the Khyber . . . [for] by comparison the
Kurram Valley, even at the season of the year, must be a paradise."*

This is yet another picture from a 'Hamilton Album'. The date is 1916, and the war
being over, my husband with the regiment he had commanded in Burma and Malaya,
had been posted to Thal in the Kurram Valley. The Kurram, though no longer part of
Afghanistan, was still 'tribal territory' and only the fort itself was part of British India.
The painting shows one of the pickets that surrounded the Fort, and this one was called
Kohat Picket, because it looked down the valley towards Kohat. The thing that looks
like a little house is, in fact, a large haystack: fodder for mules in the Fort. The hills here,
like most of the frontier hills, are treeless, but because of this they catch the light in a way
that no tree-clad hill can do, and they looked wonderful in the sunset or the dawn, and
often, on hot afternoons, they might have been made from Lalique glass. A lot of people
used to consider that Thal was a hideous spot, but it always looked beautiful to me.

from CHAPTER LIX

THAL FORT

"General Roberts, commander of the Kurram Valley Field Force . . . set out from the Kurram Forts . . ."

Robert's headquarters, during the fighting in the first months of the 2nd Afghan War, were at Thal, which is one of the Kurram Forts. This 'album picture' shows it from the outside, at evening. That whisp of smoke comes from a peculiar underground 'dump' where all the rubbish of the fort was burned, and no one seems to know who was buried in these two lonely little tombs that crown two of the nearer hillocks, or even when they were built. They have, it seems, been there 'always'.

I used poster paints for these three pictures, partly because this was the only paint I possessed when in Thal (it wasn't easy to acquire new paints in a place where there were no shops, and to get to Kohat or Peshawer necessitated a long drive, accompanied by an armed escort) but largely because only poster paint would stand out on the brown card pages of the current album. But it proved most effective in getting in the faintly dusty chalky colouring of the Kurram Valley. Perhaps my affection for Thal Fort has something to do with the fact that the war being over, I need no longer live in dread of hearing that Goff had been killed, and that our flat in the fort was the very first home of our own that we had had since we married. The others had all been brief, temporary places – often a tent — that we occupied during Goff's all too brief leaves during the war years.

from CHAPTER LIII

". . . *on hearing that Ash's goal was a valley in the Himalayas, agreed that his best plan would be to follow the caravan route to Chitral and from there across the mountains to Kashmir. 'But you cannot take your own horses,' said the Sirdar. 'They are not bred for hill work. I will give you my four mongolian ponies in their stead [they] are as strong and hardy as yaks and as sure-footed as mountain goats.*"

This might well be Ash, Juli and Gul Baz, with the Sirdar's four ponies, trekking across the passes to Chitral, and this is exactly the kind of country they would have passed through on that journey.

from CHAPTER LXVIII

NANGA-PARBAT

"Why not? We could go north . . . which will be safer at this time than trying to cross the Border and get back into British India. And from there through Kashmir and Jummu toward the Dur Khaima . . ."

Nanga-Parbat must be one of the most beautiful mountains in the world. Perhaps because there is no other peak nearby that is anything like as high, so that she stands out by herself. Many people, looking across the valley of Kashmir, have thought for a moment that there was a single high cloud in the sky, and then suddenly realised that what they were looking at was a snow peak. This painting is by my mother, who has painted Nanga-Parbat many times. She did this one on two separate pieces of paper which she stuck together, because she hadn't a larger piece with her at that time, I added the trees from a picture that I myself had done in 1947 on my last visit to Gulmarg before we all had to leave India and sail for England. Mother had just painted the mountain range and the valley, and left out the trees, but since I always think of Nanga-Parbat as one sees her from the Outer Circular road in Gulmarg, I put them in.

from CHAPTER XLVIII

This was my original sketch for a cover-design for 'The Far Pavilions'. Luck was with me, because the artist who had been asked to do the cover liked this sketch – which he could easily not have done! – and so he based his cover on it. The result was, to my mind, one of the most attractive book-jackets I have seen for a long time, and if I hadn't written the book, and knew nothing about it, I would have bought it on the strength of that cover alone. And how right he was to remove my two figures and substitute those tiny ones that give an impression of two people standing on the edge of a vast gulf and looking out hopefully toward a new and unknown world of enormous spaces and limitless horizons.

THE AUTHOR
A photograph taken in 1963
I am sitting on brocade-covered Indian-style cushions in the hall of a palace in Rajasthan, Moti Mahal, the "*Pearl Palace.*" The window behind me is the centre one of three, each one carved out of a single slab of cream-coloured sandstone, the other two so fine that they could be lace, and you can see the garden through them. I hope that one day soon I may be able to sit there again.

The following errors have regrettably occurred during the printing of this edition:

from CHAPTER III MOUNTAINS TO THE NORTH-WEST OF GULKOTE
            —for Gulmargin read Gulmarg in
            —for Gulmag read Gulmarg

from CHAPTER XXXII THE BRIDGE OF BOATS—for Peshawer read Peshawar

from CHAPTER XXXIII DAL LAKE—for takht read Takht
            —for Soloman read Solomon

from CHAPTER XXXV ANCIENT TEMPLE—for Kathiaway read Kathiawar
            —for Hahdoo read Mahdoo

from CHAPTER LVI THE KABUL RIVER—for *Lalpara* read *Lalpura*

from CHAPTER L *and* CHAPTER LX—for Kenkyns read Jenkyns
            —for Monstifi read Moustifi
            —for decorated read decorations